Back To Square One

Howard Crowhurst

epistemea

2011

Howard Crowhurst asserts his moral rights to de identified as the author of **Back to Square One** in accordance with the Copyright and Data Protection Act, 1988.

First edition
Copyright © EPISTEMEA, 2011
Cover design: David Crowhurst

ISBN : 978-2-9521871-8-3

For any information, please visit our website www.epistemea.fr
or contact
EPISTEMEA
4 avenue de l'océan
56340 PLOUHARNEL
contact@epistemea.fr

Other books by Howard Crowhurst in English:
Carnac, The Alignments: When Art and Science were One.

Back To Square One

Contents

Part One: The Event

A normal day

It was a normal day. Well, if you can call it normal when you see 15 sunrises in 24 hours and eat leek toothpaste for lunch. Gavril looked out through the panoramic window and reflected on his glorious past in the days of the USSR. More than a year spent aboard the Mir space station had made him "recordman" for weightlessness. And now, at 38, he was aboard the International Space Station, a symbol of the cordial collaboration between nations. Inevitably, he was more jaded than his team-mates.

Slowly, the stars in the window were replaced by our blue planet. To create the effect of gravity, the station was rotating slowly but Gavril weighed less than on Earth. His movements felt it. Even in an emergency, they were slow.

He turned to look at Alan, 42, a representative of American black people, euphoric about his maiden space flight. He was a last minute substitute, brought in to replace his compatriot who had had a ridiculous accident just days before take off. Alan had suddenly been thrown into the limelight. Now, he was pedalling like mad on a wheelless bike, a helmet with electrodes on his head, doing his duty with exaggerated passion.

Just behind him was Hui, the first person from China to command an ISS mission. It was only recently that his country had decided to join the international space effort after realising how much their national space programme cost. He was sitting in an armchair, reading some documents. He was relaxed.

So much for the men. But the mission also aimed

to establish parity between the sexes. The under 50 year-old housewife watches the most commercials and so she must be able, if possible, to identify with the crew.

Barisha, an Indian biologist aged 30 was in the greenhouse. Growing vegetables transform carbon dioxide into oxygen, indispensable for life on board the station. These ongoing experiments would be of great importance for future voyages to Mars. For the moment, in the greenhouses, there were tomato plants and other vegetables that require little soil and have big leaves. Even in her space overalls, she emanated something that combined sexuality and spirituality. Maybe that's what India does to you. Fortunately, the 10-day mission mean that their stay in space together was to be a short one.

Gavril was not at all troubled in the same way by Léa, who was in front of her computer. She was typing on her keyboard at a frenetic pace. Although she was French, she didn't awaken the fantasies in him which are often associated with women from her country. It was easy for him to imagine her as an aged spinster. He even wondered if she didn't already smell like one.

The ISS was more comfortable than Mir. As they could be seen by billions of TV viewers, the designers had included some stylish furniture.

The module where Gavril was standing was the centre of the social life on board. It contained a bar table near a coffee machine and 4 stools. A screen permanently displayed the date and time. Now it read GMT: December 20, 2012, 23:52. And of course there was the panoramic window, an absolute must in the category "Room With A View".

There was a sort of tunnel leading to other parts of the station. On the right, a door opened onto the toilet, which was both hygienically idiotic and unnecessary, but which made the place feel more like home. It was also somewhere you could really be on your own.

The other portion of the vessel dedicated to privacy(!) was the dormitory, containing six bunks, stacked in pairs against a wall. All the rest of the interior was for scientific purposes. Of course, they weren't there on vacation. The crackly voice of the mission director at Ground Control in Houston came out of the speakers. Despite technological advances, cosmic rays still disrupted communications. Sometimes contact with Baikonur faded completely. Russian facilities were starting to wear out.

The atmosphere in the station was a friendly enough. They managed to joke with each other in spite of massive cultural differences...

Houston: OK everyone, could you keep silent for a few moments! It's time to advertise for Pizza Hole. Alan?

Alan: Yeah!

Houston: We need you to put on your Pizza Hole jacket and catch the piece of rubber pizza in closet F.

Alan executes instructions and returns to the centre of the room to stand in front of a camera in the ceiling.

Houston: OK! Perfect. Do you remember your lines?

Alan: Yeah!

Houston: Come on, let's make a take! You ready?

Alan: Yeah!

Houston: OK. We countdown from 5 and you begin. 5-4-3-2-1

Alan: Hi everybody. Alan Greystoke on the air from the International Space Station. I just wanted to remind you that Pizza Hole manufactures quality pizzas with exceptional taste and all the nutritional intake necessary for an athlete! In addition, Pizza Hole can deliver around the world and even further.
(Big smile) Pizza Hole, we'll change your life! (Silence, frozen smile)

Houston: Cut! Awesome. Let's do another one, as a

precaution. Remember to show the slice of pizza. Go. 5-4-3-2-1

Alan: Hi everybody. Alan Greystoke on the air from the International Space Station. I just wanted to remind you that Pizza Hole manufactures quality pizzas with exceptional taste and all the nutritional intake necessary for an athlete! In addition, Pizza Hole can deliver around the world and even further. (Big smile) Pizza Hole, we'll change your life! (Silence, frozen smile)

Houston: Cut! Great! It pays the rent! Barisha, I need to remind you that tomorrow morning at 7:00 GMT, you have to advertise for Dentidelicious, the full meal with fluoride for a fast early start!

Barisha: Yes, I know!

Houston: Perfect! Well, it's time to sleep now. Good night everybody. See you tomorrow at seven o'clock.

The astronauts prepare to go to sleep, brush their teeth.

Alan: (to Gavril) Hey man, you're brushing your teeth with tomorrow's lunch. Shrimp and avocado. My favourite!

Alan and Léa say their prayers, the others don't. They get in their bunks. The lights go out. Some LEDs and a screen create a dimly lit atmosphere. You can hear the electronic background sound. Then sleep comes.

A strident alarm jerks them from their dreams, flashing lights illuminate the dark space capsule. Something's wrong !

The screen displays "December 21, 2012, 5:36 GMT.

Through stroboscopic light, everyone moves into action, talking furiously, checking systems, pressing buttons, scrutinising screens. The rhythm slows down as one by one the controls are positive. Nothing seems wrong with the station.

Hui: No imminent collision with an unknown object.

Gavril: The link is dead with Baikonur.

Hui: (ironically) It's not the first time!

Léa: With Houston as well.

Hui: That's rare.

Léa: I am trying the secondary channel ... no signal!

Through the window they can see a black sky with thousands of stars. The Earth begins to appear. Its atmosphere is full of black clouds which billow and widen.

Gavril: Look! The Earth has disappeared!

All eyes turn to the window. As the capsule rotates, the astronauts realise that their planet has become invisible. They remain silent.
Someone turns the lights on. They started checking the computer monitors.

Gavril: The atmosphere is full of sulphur and phos-
            phorus. There must have been a massive
            volcanic eruption.

Léa: No sign of unusual solar radiation.

Gavril: The seismic activity is unbelievable. It's
            gone off the scale.

Hui: Where is the epicentre?

Silence.

Gavril: Everywhere.

Hui: Let's check the external camera.

*The team is grouped around a video screen that turns
and shows images of the Earth's surface. Nothing is visible, apart from smoke.*

Alan: Christ! This is the Big One.

Hui: No, it's even bigger than the Big One. It's
            something else.

A little time passes, but no-one could say how long.

Hui: Still no visual or audible contact with the
            Earth, Gavril?

Gavril: (sobbing) I was prepared for my own death,
            but not for this.

Hui: We must be lucid and not be overwhelmed
            by emotions. At present, we have no cer-

tainties, but we must establish a plan of action. We can all survive for 18 months in the station. Two of us could survive for nearly four years. We can return to Earth in the emergency unit, but we will have to land in the ocean. For this, we will need assistance on Earth. It was always assumed that an emergency would be linked to a problem that would arise on board the station. For now, we will continue our mission and conduct our experiments, until radio contact is restored. Gavril, have you checked all the data in detail?

Gavril: (pulling himself together) According to my calculations, the Earth's axis tilt has changed more than 5 degrees. The planet is currently tilted at almost 29 degrees. The space station's orbit has been affected.

Alan cracks up.

Alan: What's the point carrying on ? Let's get down there and see what's going on.

Hui: Don't be ridiculous. They may need our help here. Down there we're useless.

Alan: Up here we're useless

Hui: If everyone's dead, we're the future of the human race !

Silence.

Alan: I was just a cog in a machine. I was happy with that. I don't think I can stand this kind of responsibility.

Hui: It's just a question of scale.

There's a tense silence. Slowly, everyone starts to real-ise what they're faced with.

Alan: Everything must be reconsidered. All our principles, beliefs, culture, habits, hang-ups, fears, desires, duties...

Gavril: It's psychological weightlessness.

Hui: Listen! We have no facts about what is happening on the surface, but as scientists, we can guess. To create such planetary pollution, dozens of massive volcanic eruptions must have happened simultaneously. This can only be caused by some kind of major upheaval inside the planet. There must have been major earthquakes leading to Tsunami and flooding. Some land masses may have been totally submerged. Many nuclear power stations must have been disrupted. The air must be unbreathable. The chances of survival in such conditions are slight. Perhaps world leaders had time to take refuge in underground shelters because volcanic incidents can be predicted. Unless the shocks come from deep down, that is. The space station, it's true, received no warning. Underground constructions could easily have been destroyed. This kind of event is unprecedented. Nowhere would be safe. Except in space.

Barisha : What about the moon ?

14

Alan :   What about the moon ?

Barisha: Has it changed orbit?

Léa: Mon Dieu!

Gavril turns to his computer. The others keep on talking. They decide they have to stay in space until the smoke clears. This will happen when all the dust particles have fallen back onto the Earth. It could take between one and three years. They take this in. They have to calculate exactly how long it will last. Léa should be able to write a computer programme to simulate the event. It'll take her six months. With help from Hui and Alan, they can bring it down to three.

Hui: Our computers are perhaps the only ones working in the world.

This idea terrifies Léa.

Léa: But computers are my life's work.

Alan: This fact seems to have hit you harder than the disappearance of humanity.

Léa: Oh God! What kind of monster have I become?

Alan: What kind of creature will you become next? You know you're going to have to repopulate the planet.

Léa: How can you joke at a time like this?
Alan: From now on, its always going to be a time like this. Wake up, Léa, I'm not joking.

Gavril:	(shouting suddenly) Hey Hui! Look at this! The moon's not in the right place! The Earth's crisis has affected the moon's orbit.
Hui:	Oh no! None of the algorithms for Léa's programme will be correct. All the bases of geophysical calculations have moved. The computer programmes which run the station and the emergency module are now wrong. The consequences are overwhelming. Gavril, you're gonna have to calculate the exact new orbit of the moon.
Gavril:	But things are unstable. I'd like to get working but there is not much I can do. We're going to have to make observations for some time before we can start to draw conclusions.
Alan:	This is unbearable. My whole life has been geared to action. Now we are powerless, overwhelmed by incredible forces we cannot predict.
Barisha:	At least we're alive.
Alan:	What does that mean?

Hui tries to regain control of the situation.

| Hui: | If the moon is moving closer to the Earth, this'll increase gravity and accelerate the dust fall. |

He is trying to bring back hope to his team members.

Gavril: The effect would be negligible. On the con-
            trary, the dust laden atmosphere will slow
            down the Earth's rotation, which will de-
            crease winds and delay the dust settling.
            Ocean currents will change and cause dra-
            matic climatic changes.

Hui: (shrugging his shoulders) We have to write
            the programme anyway, although we know
            it won't be very accurate.

Léa: I'm in agreement with that.

Secrets

The screen displays « December 28 2012, 14h22 GMT ».
Life goes on in the station. Léa, Hui and Alan work around the clock on the atmospheric dust model. Barisha concentrates on the greenhouse, the spatial agronomy project which she is developing to extend their community's life expectancy and which has now become a vital issue. Gavril, the astronomer, is observing the moon, through his computer screen, to ascertain its new orbit. The radio remains silent. The clouds of black dust still swirl around the Earth below them. Alan gets up to get a coffee. He wanders over to Barisha.

Alan: Don't you need the birds and the bees?

Barisha: (smiling) No, I get on fine without them.

Alan: You know, it's our duty to repopulate the planet. Have you thought about that?

Barisha: Yes, I have.

Silence

Alan: And what conclusions have you come to?

Barisha: Artificial insemination.

Alan: Do you really think that's the way to start over?

Barisha: It's the best I can handle for the time being. And Léa feels the same.

18

Alan: Have you two been talking?

Barisha: Of course we have. We should all talk a lot more. Everybody's closed up. You four never get your heads out of your computer screens. Is that the best way to start over?

Alan: If we don't do this, we'll never get out of here. This is all too much for anyone to take in. We just have to keep focussed on the next step or we'll go mad.

Silence

Alan: You know, Léa's nearly 40. If she's gonna have babies, she'd better not waste any time.

Barisha: A baby would never survive an Earth landing. We can't do anything up here.

Alan: We could start training. Who do you prefer as the father?

Barisha: Is it up to me to decide? If the future of humanity depends on this decision, my personal opinions are perhaps irrelevant.

Alan: Perhaps not. What would make any criterion superior to others? The future of the world depends on your subjective tastes.

Barisha: No, that can't be right. Maybe we should consider the animal kingdom. The males fight and the dominant male wins all. The survival of the fittest. That's nature's lesson.

19

Alan:	But what about feelings and intelligence? Aren't they factors that are equally important for future humans to possess? Should raw muscle and dogged determination father our descendants? Anyway, you have to think about consanguinity in future generations. As far as the females are concerned, they must both reproduce with all the males.
Barisha:	Hui must decide. He's our leader.
Alan:	Hui was chosen as a space mission commander, not as World President.
Barisha:	Listen, can you keep a secret?
Alan:	Who from ? The TV news reporters?
Barisha:	Can you?
Alan:	Trust me.
Barisha:	Léa's a virgin. She's always preferred girlfriends. This situation is impossible for her to accept. Treat her with respect.
Alan:	Oh my! So if she procreates by artificial insemination, she'll be a virgin mother. Who comes down from heaven. This is stuff creation mythology thrives on!
Barisha:	Wow! That is weird.

Gavril gets up from his seat and comes over to them.

Gavril: I overheard what you were saying.

Alan: So Hui's the only one who isn't in on the secret.

Gavril: Do you know about karma?

Barisha: I know John Lennon wrote a song about it.

Gavril: Is that all?

Barisha: Yup.

Gavril: It's the ancient law of cause and effect. It says that whatever happens to you is the result of past events and that your future is determined by your present attitude.

Alan: Sounds Newtonian.

Gavril: It's the basis of most oriental religions. It helps people think about their suffering.

Barisha: OK

Gavril: The five of us are in the same boat, right.

Alan: Right.

Gavril: Why us? What have we done, or not done, to be in this incredible situation. We're space age Noahs. Have you guys been talking to God lately?

Alan: Nope

Barisha: Me neither.

Gavril: So what's happening? Is this just a case of good, or bad, luck. Maybe there's something going on here we don't understand. You were talking about virgin birth. Can you believe that? We're something special, we have to be.

Alan: Whoah! Slow down, cowboy. Take some tranquillisers. You're leaving the road!

Gavril: Just think about it. You'll see I must be right. There was incredible selection for this mission. We're all in perfect physical condition, we're psychologically sound, we are intelligent and well read, we honour the idea of Duty. There is one of each race. We're the perfect specimens to start a new humanity.

Alan and Barisha share a worried look. Gavril walks back to his screen.

I can see clearly now

Three months have passed. The same smoky atmosphere surrounds the planet and the radio is still silent. Léa looks up from her screen.

Léa:
I don't think we can do any better. Gavril's new computations for the moon are now fairly settled. We can hope for a pretty good estimate.

Hui:
So what have we got?

Léa:
In old Earth time measurements, which of course are no longer valid, the dust should have settled in 536 days 3 hours 24 minutes and 18 seconds. Which is about 18 months.

Hui:
Thanks to Barisha's gardening, we should all be able to stay here that long.

Alan:
But what kind of state'll we be in? Another 18 months of very low artificial gravity and our muscular mass will have melted.

Léa:
And what are we going to do for all that time? Play Scrabble?

Hui:
We must maintain an intense physical activity.

Barisha:
But that'll use more oxygen.

Hui:
We must be in good physical shape to sur-

vive atmosphere entrance. And we must keep some oxygen for our arrival on Earth. The air may still be unbreathable, but we can use our spacesuits to set up water electrolysis in the sea, and then remain in the emergency module until it's safe to come out for good, without the suits. In any case, we'll have to wait until the ocean currents take us to dry land. We have enough food for a further six months.

Léa: But the emergency module's far too small for five people to live in.

Hui: We may have no choice.

Gavril: We shall be like embryos, waiting for our first breath.

Alan: And then what? Imagine we get to some island and the air is breathable. The surface'll be like the moon. Everything'll be covered in dust. There'll be no vegetation.

Barisha: We'll have to find food in the oceans. Fish will probably have thrived without their human predators. The water will be enriched by the substance from the land. We'll have to live by the sea.

Léa: Elle sera notre mer à tous.

Hui: But perhaps things'll be better than we imagine. The cloud layer will have changed the temperature and caused heavy rains. These will wash the land. It's not like the moon. The moon has no atmosphere.

Léa: I suppose we're going to have to stay together for the rest of our lives. As you say, we have no choice. So what's the point in living, if you have no freedom. I don't want this kind of life. I live for science.

Alan: Listen, we don't have to think about this all the time. We need to be joyful, we need to have fun. Maybe there are survivors. Some underground shelters are bound to have resisted. If the world leaders didn't have time to get there, the technicians who work there did. If only 50 people have survived on the planet, that changes everything. But there's no way they could get in touch with us.

Hui: Yes, Alan's right. Some people must have survived. Where there's life, there's hope. This is a new adventure, we have to rise up to it.

Gavril: Can I ask a question?

Alan: That is a question.

Gavril: We're still functioning on the old time measurement system and calendar. 24 hours a day, 7 days a week, 30 or so days a month, 12 months a year. Our clocks and computers are programmed that way. Anyone know where that comes from?

Léa: What do you mean?

Gavril:	Well, 24 for example. Why 24 hours in a day? Why not 20?
Hui:	It's just a convention.
Barisha:	No it isn't. It must be linked to a cycle. All time measurement is derived from cosmic cycles.
Gavril:	So why 24 hours?
Barisha:	I don't know. What does it matter?
Gavril:	It matters because we're going to have to re-invent a new system. If the Earth's rotation has slowed down, a day'll last longer. So will an hour, a minute and a second. The moon's orbit has become more eccentric, so its phases'll change. All the old cycles will disappear. If the days last longer, there'll be less days in a year.
Léa:	But if we change the rules, we'll lose continuity with "before".
Gavril:	We haven't changed the rules, the event has, but we have to adapt to the new cycles. It would be ridiculous to maintain a system which doesn't correspond to reality. In any case, in a few years time, we won't have watches and computers. If we want to know the date and time, we'll have to use the sky and its cycles.
Léa:	But what about Christmas and Easter and things like that? What about our own birth-

days?

Hui: And the Chinese New Year! This is the opportunity to get rid of nationalistic and superstitious habits and develop a planetary calendar based only on scientific data.

Gavril: But we're going to have to collect that data while we're up here and we have working instruments and computers.

Léa: I don't know about this. We can't just change everything. Humanity has spent thousands of years developing a coherent structure for society. We can't just make up a new one. What about laws and moral behaviour? Do you want to change those too?

Barisha: What do you mean?

Léa: Well, the Ten Commandments, for example.

Hui: The Ten what?

Léa: Thou shalt not kill, thou shalt not steal, thou shalt not covet thy neighbour's wife... (she stops.)

Alan: That's three. What are the others?

Léa: I can't remember. Anyone else know?

The other crew members look at her blankly.

Hui: Never heard of them.

Alan: Where I grew up there was "Thou shalt not walk at night in thy neighbouring gang's district" and "Thou shalt not put Coca Cola in thy Bailey's Irish Cream".

Léa: Stop it! I'm serious. We need to fix the rules we have to live by. Otherwise it's anarchy and chaos.

Barisha: We must also think about our different skills. Programming computers was pretty useful up to now, but once we're back on the surface, it won't be so easy. Are we going to try to reconstruct our old way of living, with electricity and cars and refrigerators? Who can do that? We may have to build dwelling places but we have no tools for that on board. 18 months won't be too long to think and talk and prepare for our future life on the ground.

Gavril: Who knows anything about music?

Silence

Gavril: And art, cooking, history, religion, architecture, geography, languages, etc, etc. We may be the unique sources of knowledge for our descendants. How much do we know, what is on board, how can we collate things?

Léa: Once on Earth, we must try to reach a major city and salvage all we can from the libraries and museums.

Barisha: Cities may be dangerous places. Scorpions, snakes and spiders have book lungs which resist much better in dusty environments. They eat insects. If their mammal predators have disappeared, they may have thrived.

Alan: Buildings will be unstable. Their must be pockets of gas ready to explode. There may well be a high radiation level if nuclear power plants have been destroyed. We should keep well clear of all urban structures. Our individual survival must be an absolute priority. We must leave archaeology to future generations. Our lives don't belong to us any more. They belong to the future.

Léa: So humanity's culture will be limited to ours. Pity I didn't know that when I was at school. But life'll become precious again, for at least several generations.

Gavril: And all our defects will be multiplied by thousands. If we are aggressive, mankind will be aggressive, if we are impatient, all our descendants will be impatient.

Hui: What are you talking about?

Gavril: Karma. We're a kind of filter at the top of a pyramid. If the light coming through us turns blue, the whole pyramid is blue. All our imperfections will have enormous

29

consequences. If we want to save the Human race from suffering, we must work on ourselves to become perfect beings, worthy of our primordial position. If we agree to suffer consciously, we can avoid millions of people suffering needlessly, as they did in the 20th century.

Hui: Perfect beings? Do you feel OK?

Gavril: I'm fine. Just think about it. If we quarrel amongst ourselves, our children will see and copy that way of behaving, and then their children too and so on, until it seems to be a normal thing to do. If we have sexual hang-ups (he looks at Léa), humanity'll inherit them; if we prefer plants to humans (he looks at Barisha), mankind will return to the wild; if we smother our feelings (he looks at Hui), Earth's future population will be like robots; and if we deny our spirituality (he looks at Alan), nobody'll have an aim in life.

Alan: (Looking at Gavril) And if we think we're perfect beings, we might float off into space.

Barisha: Gavril's right on this. We do have an enormous responsibility.

Alan: Yeah, we know that. But I'm me! I'm not a perfect being and I don't think I want to be.

Hui: (Looking confused) Why not?

30

Alan:	There'd be no fun in life. No pleasure.
Gavril:	You certainly have a weird idea of a perfect being. Probably linked to your stereotyped Judeo-Christian upbringing.
Alan:	Hey Man, you know nothing about my upbringing.
Gavril:	No, but I know about your country and its moral values. So many things are mixed up. Good and bad and right and wrong and sex and money and winners and losers and whites and blacks and men and women and work and leisure and pain and pleasure.
Alan:	Wow, that rhymes!
Gavril:	You have this image of a perfect being who looks likes Jesus or an E T. It just happens to be someone who does no harm and who acts consciously, who realises the consequences of his actions, and who has a vision of things which is as global, or cosmic, as possible. Someone who is capable of loving others and who doesn't live for entirely selfish reasons.
Alan:	Sounds like my dog.
Gavril:	I don't know your dog. (General laughter)
Barisha:	Gavril's got a point.
Alan:	Yeah, you said that.

Barisha: If there was ever to be a reason for people to work on themselves, to drive hatred and fear from their hearts and to love others, now's the time and we're those people. Gavril's a bit self satisfied, but you have to admit that he's not wrong.

Alan: Do I?

The crew members continue this discussion. Their mood varies between enthusiasm and despair, courage and fear, friendship and rivalry.

Part Two : A surprise

Waterworld

International Space Station: 12 months later.

Gavril: (looking through a porthole) Hey guys! Find a window. I can see the surface.

They all rush to the nearest porthole. Through a small hole in the smoke, the ocean is visible.

Alan: Oh my God! The sea has turned black.

Gavril: There's just very little light. The planet has been plunged into darkness for a year and a half.

The hole fills up with whirling smoke.

Hui: Looks pretty windy down there.

Another hole opens up in a different place.

Alan: Still the sea.

Barisha: No sign of land at all.

Hui goes back to his screen.

Hui: We're above the Atlantic ocean. We should be over the North American continent in about 6 minutes.

They stay watching the planet for some time, but the smoke remains thick.

Hui: We'll be over the USA for 10 minutes.

Time goes by but nothing else is visible. They go back to their work...

Gavril is sitting alone in a separate compartment of the station with his eyes closed. Barisha wanders over to him.

Barisha: Can we talk?

Gavril opens his eyes without speaking, smiles and nods his head towards a chair. Barisha smiles back and sits down.

Barisha: Are you meditating ?

Gavril nods.

Barisha: Can you teach me?

Gavril: (talking quietly) You're Indian and you never learnt to meditate?

Barisha: Me and 500 million other Indians. Just like Europeans who don't know how to pray.

Gavril: Do you know how to pray?

Barisha: You close your eyes and you talk to your-self? Can you teach me to meditate? I can see it helps you handle this situation and I need help. It seemed a thing of the past when I was a kid, but now it seems to me that it may be a thing of the future, if there's going to be one.

| Gavril: | There's bound to be a future, it's just that humans may not be in it. Listen, I'm willing to pass on to you what I have learnt, but there are conditions. |

Barisha raises her eyebrows.

| Gavril: | You must agree to keep it to yourself until I give you permission to transmit to others. |

| Barisha: | Why? |

| Gavril: | You must agree. But you don't have to answer now. Take your time. Think about it. |

| Barisha: | Can't you explain why? |

| Gavril: | No, I can't because you can't understand. You have to trust me. If you don't trust me, I can't teach you. |

| Barisha: | Who do take yourself for? Do you think you're superior? |

| Gavril: | You asked me for help. If you don't want it, no problem. |

| Barisha: | I'm sorry. This is rather difficult for me. I turned my back on my father's religion and I suppose I must feel guilty about it. |

| Gavril: | What I know and do has nothing to do with religion. |

| Barisha: | Where does it come from then? |

Gavril:	That's another condition. You must not seek to discover the origin of what you learn. That is simple curiosity and has no place in this work. You may ask me, however, as many questions you wish about the work itself and your experiences with it.
Barisha:	Are there any other conditions?
Gavril:	Not for the time being. There may be later on, that depends on you.
Barisha:	But if I agree to these conditions, I'll have to be deceitful to the others. I shall be obliged to hide things from them.
Gavril:	Are you hiding nothing from them now? I can only share what I know with people who want it and appreciate it. Otherwise, it would harm them and me. Those are the rules. I didn't invent them. That's just the way it is. But if you need more time to think, don't worry. That's one thing we have plenty of for the moment. I know you've been working up to asking me this for months already.
Barisha:	How do you know that?
Gavril:	I could see it in your eyes.

They hear Alan calling them. There's excitement in his voice. They hurry to him.

Alan:	China's disappeared.

Barisha:	What?
Alan:	Look through the window. We should be flying over China.

Barisha and Gavril peer through the porthole. There is a large hole in the smoke and only the sea is visible.

Barisha:	Our calculations that must be wrong. The Earth's rotation has slowed down.
Alan:	The truth is that for the moment we've only seen water. It's like Waterworld with Kevin Costner. Even the film was a catastrophe.
Barisha:	It's too early to draw any conclusions. We'll have to be able to see the surface a little better.
Alan:	If we have to wait here until the Earth comes out of the sea, we going to have to draw lots to decide who stays alive. By the way, how's your work on the plants coming along Barisha? Are your kind vegetable friends eating all our nasty carbon dioxide emissions.?
Barisha:	(hesitating) I haven't yet spoken to Hui about this.
Alan:	You love red tape don't you?
Barisha:	(angrily) Yes! That's what I'm like you see. I believe in hierarchy. We need it. (She stares at him defiantly). Everybody can't be the leader.

Alan:	No, and we're not all sheep either.
Gavril:	It is not possible to recognize in others qualities that we do not possess ourselves.
Alan:	(to Barisha) OK. He's on repeat mode.
Barisha:	It sounds like common sense to me. If someone has never tasted strawberries, they can't imagine their fragrance. Similarly, a miser cannot recognize generosity, even if it hits him in the face.
Gavril:	Right. And it also works for defects. If I have no hate in me, I can't understand someone else's hatred. That's what makes the lives of small children and animals so difficult.
Alan:	In other words, you gotta keep ya mouth shut and mindlessly obey the boss's orders.
Gavril:	Why mindlessly? Obedience comes from the word 'listen'. In reality, obedience is the only way I can escape the dictates of my ego. By submitting to someone else's will, I can see my resistance and fears. This person inside, who wants to control everything, can't hide. He gets angry, he repeats incessantly "what about me?" . Except that his idea of control is pure illusion. He controls nothing. He can die at any moment. If, instead, he learns to obey, he opens up to the universe. This is the basis of any relationship of master to disciple.
Alan:	And Houston decides who is the master?
Gavril:	Why not? Every human being can teach us something, if we open up to them.
Alan:	(raising his voice) What you say is pernicious and dangerous.

Gavril: For who?

Alan: For free thought, for spontaneity, for love
            ...

Gavril: Wouldn't you prefer to talk about some-
            thing you know about?

Alan: (yelling) Hey! Who do you think you are,
            you fucking asshole!

*Alan throws himself at Gavril, screaming, although his ac-
tion is slowed by the weakness of gravity. Gavril dodges
at normal speed and Alan is projected into the void. He
turns to attack, but all his movements are in slow motion
while Gavril's are at normal speed. He howls in frustra-
tion. Barisha observes with astonishment. Hui arrives
through the tunnel. He advances toward Alan.*

Hui: What's going on here? What's the matter
            with you Alan? Pull yourself together!

*Alan screams like a child in a tantrum He throws him-
self on Hui who cannot avoid him. They both fall to the
ground (gently). They roll across the room. Léa enters
from the tunnel. With the others, she grabs Alan's arm
to restrain him. Alan collapses into tears, he has trouble
breathing. Barisha pulls out a syringe from the closet,
and while the others hold Alan, she gives him an injec-
tion. His body shakes for a moment, then relaxes. He is
lying unconscious.*

Léa: What happened to him? What you have
            done?

Hold your breath!

The screen displays "April 16, 2014, 8:15 GMT".
Alan is lying on a couch. He's asleep .Léa and Barisha are having coffee together.

Léa: Do you think he's still asleep?

Barisha: Yes. And will be for a few more hours. (Pause). Still no sign of land. In fact, we can't see much at all. (Silence) Léa, when Alan freaked out, what were you two doing ?

Léa: What?

Barisha: I think you heard me. Hui took a lot of time to show up, and you took even more, despite the shouting here! Tell me the truth. I'm not stupid.

Léa: But what are you insinuating? I don't have to justify myself, especially not to you.

Barisha: What does that mean?

Léa: Do you think we're not aware of your relationship with Gavril?

Barisha: We?

Léa: Yes, well, you know what I mean.

Barisha: Not really.

Léa: (pause) What's happening here? Every-
           one's on edge. Is there a gremlin in the
           station or what? Only Hui remains calm.

Barisha: That's normal. He was well conditioned in
           China. He's a real machine.

Léa   Barisha! What's come over you?

Barisha: And if this was the real me now? Maybe it's
           just the coating of my "education" crack-
           ing. I don't want to pretend. I want to say
           what I think. Alan is a baby. Hui is an ex-
           tinct volcano. Gavril's lost in space. Is there
           a real man aboard this damn ship? We're
           not going to repopulate the earth with
           wankers like that.

Léa: You can't reject everything like that. I
           thought you liked Gavril enormously.

Barisha: He's spent too much time in space. (She
           leans towards Léa and speaks softly). He
           is not normal. He defies the laws of grav-
           ity. That's what blew Alan. It is downright
           weird.

Hui arrives through the tunnel. Barisha recovers.

Hui: It seems you wanted to tell me about your
           experiences with the vegetables?

Barisha: Did Gavril tell you that?

Hui: Yes.

42

Barisha:	It's none of his business.
Hui:	But is it true or not?
Barisha:	Yes. I have results I do not understand. The level of oxygen in the station is decreasing much more slowly than expected.
Hui:	(smiling) It's rather good news.
Barisha:	(serious) It is an anomaly and, as such, it worries me. I have a monitor on our oxygen consumption with the station's reprocessing system, and another on the plants' oxygen production, and the two sides of the equation are not equal. It is as if there was another source replenishing our oxygen atmosphere from inside. It scares me.
Hui:	Frankly, I don't understand you women. This is the best information I could imagine, and you're not happy with it. You most certainly have a problem with one of your devices. Your plants must be extremely efficient. It is a great success for your scientific approach. This'll open the way for a new space age. You'll be a Nobel Prize nominee.
Barisha:	(aside to Léa) You see what I mean. Listen, Hui! I checked my whole system at least ten times. There is no malfunction. It is physically impossible for the quantity of plants growing in the vessel to produce the volume of oxygen found, unless the basic laws of physics have completely changed.

Hui: But there must be a rational explanation.

Barisha: That's my opinion too. In the meantime, we have to discover it. But I've not given you the figures yet.

Hui: Go ahead.

Barisha: I told you that the level of oxygen has not decreased as expected. In fact, in recent days, it has increased.

Hui and Léa: What?

Barisha: I wonder, also, if there is not some relationship with the crew's increased nervousness. We seem to have more energy than before and everybody's doing things to try to release it.

Hui and Léa share a look that does not escape Barisha.

Barisha: (to Léa) See! I told you that something was going on between you. I suppose your choice is no surprise. You are as stuck up as he is. Go on, please don't mind me! Procreate! There'll be enough air for two more lungs. (She laughs hysterically, then bursts into tears.) I am tired of this shit ... I want to go home ... I can't take this any more ...

Léa puts her arm around her, but Barisha is inconsolable. Léa shares looks of astonishment and concern with Hui. Barisha gets up and goes down the tunnel to lie down on her berth. Hui and Léa stay at the table.

Léa: Do you want a cup of coffee, tiger?

Hui: With pleasure, baby. It'll make a break from all these crazy jerks. In fact, I wanted to tell you it was great last night. You're amazing, kitten.

Léa: You too, leopard. (She licks his cheek, arched like a cat). Do you think you'll be able to arrange a zero gravity party, for just the two of us? I can't wait. We might as well make the most of it. Maybe we could give injections to everyone or put sleeping pills in the herbal tea? How can they be so boring! (Pause) And so stupid too. It was a good idea to tell Barisha I was a lesbian and a virgin. It's like they all went blind. (She puts a finger in Hui's mouth. He sucks it with pleasure. She begins to unzip his overalls. Hui stop her.)

Hui: Later, baby. Hold your fire. We gotta stay low profile for now. We still need them. While they're fighting amongst themselves, it gives us space. In a few hours, we'll have the world to ourselves, just for us two.

Léa: Yeah, and due to the oxygen anomaly, they'll be able to play together for decades and eat green tomatoes. A true colony. Lost in space. (She laughs). And meanwhile, thou shalt be my Adam and I shall be your Eve.

Hui: You are sure about your calculations?
Léa: I'm certain. In 15 days, everything'll be back to normal down there. We'll take a

flight path that will land us in the water off Mexico and from there, the new ocean currents'll carry us to Florida. With the new tilt of the Earth's axis, we'll have an ideal temperate climate.

Hui: Have you considered the possibility that something may happen to me, and that you would be alone in the world?

Léa: Yes, I have. I would put an end to my life and humanity in general. But it'll not happen. It makes no sense. And since it is obvious to me that all this is intentional, if it should happen anyway, then "inshala". Our story is already so incredible. We could have died on Earth, like dogs, with the other seven billion. But no! We were above it all.

Hui: I love you, Léa. You are a truly an amazing woman. (They kiss). This whole experience really helped you blossom. This disaster won't have taken place for nothing. (Thoughtful silence). It's strange though, this business with the oxygen.

Hurt feelings

The screen displays May 3, 2014, 3:10 GMT.
All the astronauts are asleep in their bunks except Gavril, who is sitting cross legged on the ground in the dark, near the coffee table.

Gavril: Here we are. The big day has arrived. In a few minutes Hui and Léa will wake up. They'll go to the airlock leading to the emergency unit. They'll put on their airtight spacesuits. Then they'll go into the emergency unit. Only Hui, as mission commander, knows the necessary codes for such an operation. They'll disconnect from the station and they'll both fly down to our beloved planet Earth. They'll abandon here their three colleagues, Barisha, Alan and myself to an unbearable fate with no hope of rescue. Why will they do that? Because they believe that 5 people could never survive in the emergency unit for the time it takes to reach the coast. In fact, 5 people would have to stay lying down constantly. It would be impossible to prepare correct food. There would not even be room to install the electrolysis system needed to manufacture oxygen from seawater. The air, essential to survival if the atmosphere, is too laden with dust. Insofar as they consider Barisha, Alan and I to be emotionally unstable, they think that we could never withstand such conditions and that the failure of one of the three of us could cause the loss of the entire team. They are taking with them some solar panels, which Hui has quietly dismantled, and computers containing the entire main memory of the station. This extra weight is another reason which necessitates a reduction in the number of persons permitted on board the emergency module. For without solar panels, no electrolysis, so no drinking water. Although Léa did not at all agree, Hui would have taken Barisha in his luggage. It is true that she is pretty. But they concluded that Barisha, too dominated by her feelings unfortunately, would never have accepted such a proposal, and that the mere fact of asking her would have aborted the whole project. Hui is certain that there are survivors on Earth. He knows, though he has ever said, that shelters were built to withstand all that the planet has endured. These shelters are waterproof, indestructible, even in case of nuclear explosion, equipped with everything needed to survive for decades. However, he was able to get the other members of the crew to believe the opposite. He developed his plan in the minutes that followed the discovery of the disaster. It was immediately clear that his own survival was a priority and should determine each decision. They have decided to leave immediately because Léa is no longer young and should lose no time before having babies. Léa admired Hui for his great insight and was well aware that as captain, he was the only one able to operate the emergency unit. They have really thought of everything ...

or almost, because they could not know that a solar storm of incredible power, which occurred during my stay aboard the Mir space station, left me with abnormal lucidity. Unfortunately for them, and for me, I followed step by step the construction of their diabolically selfish plan. I watched all their trickery as it happened. I was plunged into the swamp of their disgusting machinations. And I said nothing. Not a word. No signs. For months I suffered in silence. My pain was too great, my despair too deep for me to act, even if only through words. Although the human race was threatened with extinction, these two people were plotting to eliminate 60 percent of the survivors. No remorse crossed their conscience. They continued their Nazi logic in peace. Also, nobody on board was really sensitive to my point of view. Barisha was a bit at first and then she changed. I felt totally alone. But now? ... This is my last chance. Will I be able to act? ... What could push me to intervene, to stop the process? An instinct for survival? (Pause) I'm too disgusted to want to continue living. After all the billions of dead, how can I attach importance to my own little life? I do not want to die but I don't want to live either. To start all over again on a destroyed planet? To swim continuously against the current of human stupidity? It's too much for me. I'm tired of it. (Pause) So? Why should I stop them? ... A sense of injustice could move me, maybe. Yes, I have always been sensitive to injustice. But my appreciation is subjective. Who am I to decide what is right and what is not? Only God can judge. If God does not intervene, why should I? I know he has a world to manage, but this is the question of the survival of humankind on Earth ... Yes, indeed, no great loss, you may say. So ... I only have a few more seconds to make up my mind ... Not to act is an action itself ...

Hui gets out of his bed in a dim light. Slowly, he shakes Léa to wake her. She gets up in silence. Both walk on tiptoe and disappear into the emergency tunnel. Gavril can hear them putting their spacesuits on. Then he hears someone, obviously Hui, hitting a key code. Each key beeps. Suddenly all the lights come on and lively music blasts out of the speakers.

Houston: Come on, wake up in there! Game over. Wake up!

Léa and Hui rush back from the tunnel in their space suits, staring in bewilderment. Alan and Barisha leap out of their bunks. Gavril is recovering from his sitting position and moves awkwardly towards the others.

Barisha: What's happening? Houston is that you? Are there many survivors?

Houston: (laughs) Welcome to Loft in Space, voted the best show on the planet in 2013. Hui, Léa, Gavril, Barisha, Alan, go and stand in front of the main camera, so we can see you all well. That's it! The adventure ends here for you all. Hui typed the code and the story ends. Bravo. You were great.

Alan: What is this crap? Gavril, is this another one of your tricks?

Houston: No Alan, you are hearing the voice of Houston. Your story has been followed for 15 months and a half by more than 3 billion viewers worldwide. Look out of the window.

The five astronauts turn to the panoramic porthole. Before their eyes is an image of clouds slowly fading, being replaced by that of our well known blue planet. They turn to each other, wide eyed. A thunder of applause and cheers can be heard in the speakers. It's a standing ovation. Hui falls to his knees. Houston's jubilation is in total contrast with the astronauts dismay. It's as if time has stopped.

Part Three : Coming Down

Way Out

About an hour later, Léa is sitting on a stool in front of the toilet door.

Léa:　　　　　Listen Hui, you'll have to come out some time... You can't stay in there forever... Someone else'll need to go...

She shrugs and sighs.

Léa:　　　　　The TV viewers agreed with you that the others would not have been up to an Earth landing. Your decisions were accepted by 78% of the people.

Hui:　　　　　(muffled voice from inside the toilet) That only makes it worse. It's probably mostly the Chinese, who vote by blind patriotism. This is too much for me. I'll never go back down among all those idiots. I realise now that I was pleased they'd all been wiped out!

Léa:　　　　　But you're not going to solve anything by staying in the toilet.

Hui:　　　　　It is the only place without cameras. I can't stand being looked at. Leave me alone! Go away!

Léa:　　　　　Alan and Gavril have covered all the cameras and cut radio contact. We're going to solve our problems among ourselves, without outside eyes or ears.

Hui: They'll kill us!

Léa: With their bare hands? I mean, it wouldn't
            be very discreet. Can you imagine Hercule
            Poirot in the station? (She takes on a deep
            voice.) "The culprit is in this room." Any-
            way, Hui, for security reasons, there's a key
            to open the toilet from the outside. If you
            don't come out of your own accord, they'll
            come and get you. Be a man. Don't leave
            me alone to deal with all the criticism.
            (There's a long silence) ... We must stay
            together. We must decide together how
            we can avenge Houston's psychological
            rape. There must be people on earth who
            were shocked by the principle of this TV
            programme. (Hui remains silent) ... Even
            if we did sign papers which waved all our
            rights, including the event of death, we've
            been victims of treachery. We must defend
            ourselves.

*Suddenly, there is the thud of a body falling to the
ground.*

Léa: My God! Hui, Hui, answer me!

*Silence. Léa bangs on the bathroom door but there's no
answer. Gavril comes running in, then Barisha and Alan
(in slow motion).*

Gavril: What's happening?

Léa: Hui's collapsed in the toilet. He's not an-
            swering.

Gavril goes to a cupboard and opens the door.

Gavril: Shit! The key's disappeared. He's thought of everything.

Alan: He's not going to escape from us like this. I learned some stuff in my youth.

He opens a drawer and pulls out a wire. After several seconds fiddling in the lock, the toilet door opens. Hui is lying on the floor inside. The two men pull him out and carry him to the greenhouse, where Barisha has medical equipment. She puts her ear to his chest.

Barisha: His heart's stopped beating! Help me with the defibrillator.

The men push a crate on wheels. Barisha applies two electrodes to Hui's chest. There's a cracking noise and the lights dim in intensity as Hui's body shakes violently. She gives him mouth to mouth and then puts the electrodes back on his chest. She repeats this 3 times. Hui remains inert. Barisha look at the others.

Barisha: He's dead.

Léa: No, he can't be. Two minutes ago, he was speaking to me quite normally.

Barisha: He must have swallowed a fast poison. He'd planned it.

Gavril: But he'd do anything to survive! I don't believe it. This is another of his tricks. Recheck! Plug him into a machine.

Barisha installs electrodes on Hui's chest and brain. On
56

the screens, flat lines appear.

Barisha: Electrocardiogram: no signal; electroencephalogram: no signal. No breathing. He's clinically dead. It's too late. The brain is irreparably damaged. Gavril, I'm sorry, but this is no trick. The four astronauts look at the body, paralyzed.

Alan: Shit! He managed to escape, the bastard.

Gavril: This puts us in a real mess.

Alan: What?

Gavril: We voluntarily cut all ties with the Earth. We covered the cameras and cut radio contact. 10 minutes later, Hui dies. We had excellent reasons for killing him. If you're on a jury in court, what would you conclude?

Alan: I don't believe it! I thought he'd done us the worst damage possible, and now he's made it even worse.

Léa: He didn't mean to. He felt terribly humiliated, ashamed. He couldn't face the world.

Alan: Yup! As usual, he only thought about himself.

Léa: But he's dead! Show some kind of respect.

Alan: Hitler's dead too. That doesn't make him a hero.

Barisha: Listen, don't panic. If we remain united and tell the truth, they can't condemn us all.

Gavril: You still have a lot of illusions about our world, despite what it's done to you. We're gonna be the OJ Simpsons of space, except that this time, they'll get it wrong the opposite way round, to make up. I can already imagine the tone of indignation in the prosecutor's voice as he says "For Christ's sake, it was only a game!." We'll look like bad losers and Hui'll be a victim. This story could even be seen as a Russian-American conspiracy against China and trigger off an international incident. The planet has entered a new era, the era of space crime.

Léa: But legally, which country's laws are we subject to? Do we risk the death penalty?

Alan: Right! Let's get thinking. There's no way that I'm gonna pay for the death of that rat. We've gotta find a solution. Léa, you'll just have to confess to the crime. You owe us that much. Besides, if you refuse, I'll kill you too. What have I got to lose? Gavril, Barisha, say something.

Gavril: About an hour ago, I decided to go silently to my own death, letting our "colleagues" act without intervening. I have not changed my position. I do not want to act as a judge because I do not trust my own notion of justice. If there are forces beyond our own perception, let them handle this situation. I put myself in their hands.

Alan: I don't believe it! You don't wanna defend
             yourself? Weren't you a soldier once.

*Suddenly, Hui's body shakes. He opens his eyes and
leans up on his elbows. He looks at the astronauts, one
after another, with a smile on his lips.*

A passing angel

The five astronauts are seated around the table. They're drinking coffee.

Alan: If you think you'll cool us down by dying and coming back to life, you're wrong, buddy. Although I must admit, it's was an incredible act.

Hui: I can assure you that I did not intend to return. The angel forced me to.

Léa: What?

Hui: I was actually dead. I was hovering over my body and I saw you trying to bring me back to life. Then I felt a strange presence beside me and a voice inside said "You'll not get out of it like this."

Gavril: I said that.

Hui: No, Gavril. When you said it, there was hatred in your voice. The being who spoke those words was full of love. He explained simply, without reproach, that suicide was not a solution to my problem and that everything would start over again. He told me "Your time has not yet come. You'll have to go back. " He radiated so much light that I could barely look at him. Then, suddenly, my whole life flashed before my eyes, like a 3D movie, but I also felt the effects of my actions on others. It was like I was the others. I was filled with shame, seeing all the suffering around me that I generated through my selfishness and my lies. It was terrible. I saw how all my actions were devoid of love. I had no idea of time. All the details of my life were revealed, hidden things I thought that nobody would ever know, were displayed openly in front of that being. Yet he did not judge me. I felt stupid, very stupid, but it seemed to amuse him. And then, towards the end, I saw you, Gavril. I felt the path you've travelled and all the suffering caused by your inability to share your experience with others. I saw how this suffering can be transformed into anger and bitterness, or if it is digested, into love and wisdom. And I felt the fragility of your situation. Then I woke up in my body. You were all around me.

Gavril starts sobbing and his body shakes. Barisha puts an arm around him. Gradually he calms down. When he looks up, there's a smile on his lips, similar to Hui's. Léa and Alan are stunned. There is a long silence.

Gavril: Thanks, Hui. That's the help I needed. This being that you saw is a part of you. That's why his voice came from within you. The enormous tension in this station's atmosphere has been resolved through your experience. We are at the dawn of a new era for us and for humanity.

Alan: Woah! Not so fast! What's happening here? Léa, you're very rational, what do you think of this?

Léa opens her mouth but no sound comes out. Then we heard a little girl's voice.

Léa: He was dead. We've all saw him. He began to turn blue. Then he got up. Then ... then ... and now he's different. Do you agree with me?

The others nod their head in agreement. Léa continues as if she were talking to herself.

Léa: It is clear that he has changed. Hui is not at all the same.

Alan puts his arm around Léa, who is visibly upset.

Gavril: It all makes sense now. Through this program, Loft in Space, we are now the most famous humans on the planet Earth. We have a huge field of influence. This episode, perhaps the vilest and most shameful of the human species, in which its own destruction is staged to entertain the crowds, is the starting point for a revival. It's when you've sunk right to the bottom that you can push hard to go back up.

Hui: Do you have a plan?

Gavril: We have to play it very subtly. The powers that be do not want a radical change. The deeper people sleep, the easier they can be controlled. Fortunately for us, Houston saw nothing of what happened. They believe that we hate each other and that we're settling our debts.

Alan: Don't we hate each other? Everything seems to have worked out very quickly for you. Have you already forgotten that they were going to abandon us, without any hope of rescue, to a slow and agonizing death?

Gavril: That was then. You don't think that Hui faked his death?

Alan: No.

Gavril: In that case, we must assimilate what happened. This changes everything. An angel came to purify it all. Hui is transformed. Revenge is meaningless and time consuming...

Alan: What about Léa? She's still the same.

All eyes turn to Léa.

Léa: What? How can we be the same after all this? Do you feel the same, Barisha? You haven't said anything. And you, Alan?

Barisha: (after a pause) You know that I was tuned in to Gavril's ideas. Then, after the bizarre incident with Alan, I got scared and morally betrayed Gavril. But Hui's revival, which I saw with my own eyes, has exploded all my certainties. Why am I afraid of things that I do not understand? It's not a scientific attitude. But I can see that the foundations on which I built my beliefs have huge flaws. It's become clear to me that there are realities that go far beyond our small

63

mental capacity. And these realities, which up to now have scared me, and scare everyone in positions of power, seem now more important than my little ego. What has the spirit of vengeance to do with this reality? Gavril goes fast, it's true, but I'm starting to understand why.

Alan: For those of us who understand less quickly, could you explain more slowly, Gavril?

Gavril: What we have lived through up here for the last 15 months has shown us both the fragility of the human species and the magnitude of his accomplishments. The idea of having to start again was almost unbearable.

Alan: Yes.

Gavril: But humanity is lost in excessive materialism. Everything is linked consumption and accumulation of wealth. If humans were immortal, this attitude would make sense, but they aren't. Terrestrial life does not last long and, therefore, collecting material things does not make sense.

Hui: When you see what I just experienced, then it becomes obvious.

Gavril: Even so, we were ready to restart everything and we saw all the traps. The question is: Is a new beginning possible with the earth's population still alive? Where are the obstacles? In recent years there have been many disaster films that attract a large audience and I have often wondered if people felt the need to start over but only believed it possible after almost total destruction. Do you follow me? Is it possible for human existence to work properly, without going through a reset?

Hui: Those who hold power are ready to survive disaster and then rebuild the same world. But it makes no sense. My country has tried a new model, but it has become just like the others.

Gavril: It's because your new model lacked spirituality.

Alan: There have been many attempts based on spirituality. Christianity led to the Inquisition. Everything ends up being corrupt.

Gavril: Wait a minute. We're losing track. Let's look at things differently. How do you see your life once back down on Earth? Do you think you can live like before?

Alan: It's true that the organizers of Loft in Space didn't give a shit about us. Now the show's over, they'll move on to the next one. I wonder how future astronauts will be recruited. Our adventure was so successful that they'll probable want to do it again. Not to mention the money they earned at our expense.

Gavril: In my opinion, as we are speaking, they are preparing their defence. They expect an all out attack on our part to get our

65

share. They think we think like them. But I do not think like them and I have a plan.

Hui: Go ahead, spit it out!

Gavril: Hui, you said that you didn't want to come back among us, but that light being forced you to do so.

Hui: Right.

Gavril: So would you be ready to go back?

Hui: Pardon?

Gavril: Would you agree to commit suicide again, but this time, in front of billions of viewers?

Léa: Are you serious?

Alan: That's insane!

Barisha: No it's not. It's genius!

Léa: But what if the angel doesn't come back? What if Hui doesn't resurrect?

Gavril: We need to think about a plan of action in both cases. If Hui commits suicide on live television and is pronounced clinically dead by doctors and then he comes back to life, earthly life couldn't go continue in the same way. The shock would be immense because modern communication would give power to the event which Christ himself was denied. It would be a giant spiritual tsunami!

Léa: But why should Hui do that? It's your idea, you just have to try it yourself.

Gavril: First, it isn't certain that I have a guardian angel. Second, Hui's suicide will be seen as an act of remorse after terribly selfish behaviour. It'll be a strong message to all those who agreed with his action. Third, if he rises from the dead, the new Christ would be Chinese, hitting the heart of the biggest obstacle to the spiritual renewal of the planet.

Hui: Wait a minute. I'm not the new Christ. On the contrary, I saw in an instant the distance I have to cover on the path to spiritual perfection. I understand your idea. I think it's good and I'm not opposed to it, because now, I'm not afraid of death. But even if I was forced to return again, I can't play the Saviour. The whole crew is concerned.

Alan: Here we go. The commander's taken control. Listen, don't count on me. I already have a life.

Barisha: Hui, are you suggesting that we all take our own lives and hope that we all come back to life?

Hui: No, not at all. I wanted to say that if I returned again to my body, everyone should participate in the after effects. If 5 senior scientists support the existence of mind independently from the body, if we are welded in our desire to see radical changes in earthly life with a return to love as a fundamental value, in short, if we return united from our space experience, despite our different cultures and beliefs, then we show a model for the future. We'll be living proof that it's a possibility, despite the reasons that everyone knows we have to hate each other.

Léa: But why do you have to die for that?

Gavril: Because the world needs a big shock. Everyone is asleep to the truth that we have just experienced, the existence of a superior mind, the purpose of earthly life.

Léa: (yawning) Exactly, you yourself doubt the existence of your own guardian angel. I suggest instead that Hui talks of his experience, and then you kill yourself to show your own faith.

Gavril: Hey! Our goal is not to push people to commit suicide en masse!.

Barisha: (looking very tired) I don't think we can oblige higher forces to achieve our own goals, however high they may be. In reality, we have no control. Ever since we've set foot in this station, we've been constantly manipulated, either from below by Houston or from above, by whoever. Isn't the lesson to be learned from all this that we should try to adapt to events and use them to better understand the world and the cosmos, rather than trying to become manipulators ourselves? (She yawns) It's exactly the profound mistake of modern science which "corrects" oversights or "mistakes" in nature.

Gavril: (rubbing his eyes) So you think nothing should be done.

Barisha: It's funny. I thought that was your position. Didn't you say "who am I to judge?". The problem is the illusion of doing. But listen, I feel exhausted. I think my nervous system's falling apart. I'm going to bed.

Alan: Yeah, me too.

He gets up but falls over. Barisha, looking worried, staggers to her instruments.

Hui: What's happening?

Barisha: There's almost no oxygen! Houston has intervened to force us to reconnect.

Gavril: The bastards!

Hui: No anger Gavril. Love, always love ...

He gets up, moves his chair and climbs to remove the tissue that's concealing the camera. He smiling into the lens, then goes to the control panel to restore radio contact.

Hui: Okay, Houston. All systems go. My diarrhea is over. I've taken command. You can give us air.

The art of war

The ISS is plunged into darkness. The astronauts are sleeping in their bunks. An alarm rings. The lights come on.

Houston: Hello everybody! Wake up. It's time to come home.

Hui: (sleepy) What? What did you say?

Houston: In the next few hours, the replacement team will be arriving at the station. Your mission is over, but before you leave, I would like us all to have a little chat. Come on, get up!

The astronauts emerge from their berths, stretch and move towards the table and the coffee machine. They settle around the table.

Houston: Okay, Gavril? Not too many revolutionary ideas?

Gavril: Hey? What's the matter? You got a problem?

Houston: No, just a joke. You are Russian, after all.

Hui glances at Gavril to calm him down.

Houston: Good. We are not unaware that the show, Loft in Space, could be considered to be offending and that there may be a spirit of revenge among some of you. We want to start by telling you that your participation in this

70

program has saved space adventure from bankruptcy. Having heard of the exorbitant additional costs that the building of international space station had generated, some unscrupulous people approached the 16 countries participating in this project. Their advisors suggested this show as the solution to the financial problem, although it was shameful for science. All the governments agreed as many of them were in great need of assets. The general public does not understand why we are spending fortunes on the conquest of space, while countries are experiencing major financial crises. The leaders saw this as a solution to popularize space, which has turned out to be true. And the result has exceeded the wildest dreams. You can't imagine the effect produced by this program. The whole world has been talking about it. The planet was united by your adventure. People were asking themselves the same questions that you were, they were living the same existential experience. Groups formed, with debates on global Internet. Gavril has millions of followers who expect him to come down from heaven to save the Earth. His final monologue, subtitled in over 100 languages, was followed live by the highest number of viewers ever in the history of mankind: a little over 3 billion 156 million .For some people, it was four o'clock in the morning. The show was a profound shock to the human race, including its leaders. Millions of people were crying in front of their televisions, transfixed by the intense feeling of loneliness that emanat-

71

ed from Gavril, sharing the suffering of one who sees the lies and the cheating of others, but who does not yield to violence and is willing to die if necessary. And it was not a movie! It was true, as true as truth can be. Officials on TV stations cancelled the advertisements. Everyone was hanging on the outcome of your adventure, as if the future of Earth itself depended on it.

Léa: But people must hate me! Hui and I were the incarnation of absolute evil.

Houston: It's not true. Because it's human. It's not as if you had wanted to create a holocaust!. Everyone followed the story from the beginning and nobody would have liked to have been in your situation. However, obviously there are some extremists who would like to murder you.

Léa: My God!

Houston: We'll ensure your safety. But if you show that the events have been forgiven, if you show you're united, despite everything that happened, it'll be the best gift you can give to the world. If it is war amongst you, the international repercussions could be catastrophic.

Alan: That's incredible! Whatever happens, we have an enormous responsibility on our shoulders!

Houston: You must realize that you are the most famous people on Earth since the beginning of human history. Your lives can never be the same. The slightest of your actions will have incalculable consequences, just as you had imagined when you thought you were the last survivors. This is not a global catastrophe, but the result is the same. When you return to Earth, you'll not find the same planet that you left. Something has changed profoundly. Just look how I'm talking!

Gavril: I don't want to go back down there. I'm staying here!

Houston: Don't be silly, Gavril.

Gavril: I'm not kidding. I'm no messiah. How do we know that what you're saying is true? So far you have never stopped cheating on us. You made us suffer unbearable psychological pressure.

Houston: You were selected for this. You said it yourself. Besides, you all look great.

Barisha: I want to talk to my husband.

Houston: (Silence) Now? It's three o'clock in the morning in India.

Barisha: I don't think he's asleep. Anyway, it can't wait. Call him, then pass me the call.

Houston: (Silence) I'm afraid it is not possible, Barisha.

Barisha: Why not?

Houston: Your husband is in jail.

Barisha: What?

Houston: When he discovered the truth about your space mission, he wanted to end the program and filed a complaint for the unlawful detention of persons against their will. He lost his case because the reality show was implicitly included in your contracts. So he freaked out and physically attacked a television producer, causing him serious injuries. He received a sentence of 2 years in prison. He's still inside, because he hasn't behaved particularly well during his incarceration.
            Listen, I prefer to tell you the truth. I'm really sorry, but we can't do anything for him. No one is above the law.

Alan: Bullshit! It's really disgusting! You're acting like a victim but you're an accomplice. I agree with Gavril. We're gonna occupy the station until Barisha's husband is let out of prison. Then we'll see if you powerless to intervene.

Houston: Be reasonable! You know that we control the station.

Alan: Are you threatening to kill us? You've already stolen our lives. What about my wife? And my children? Are they are in prison too? Can I contact them?

Houston: You have touched on a delicate subject, Alan. We don't want to hassle you or make your life more difficult. You've already had much to take in.

Alan: What? Has something happened to my wife and my kids?

Houston: No, don't worry Alan. They are all in good health. But you seem to forget that your wife followed all your actions online. You had only just realised she was dead when you started making unequivocal proposals to Barisha. You can imagine that she was angry. In fact, there is a lawsuit waiting for you when you land.

Alan: I don't believe you. I know my wife and she also knows me very well. She wouldn't act like that.

Houston: Sometimes you think you know people, but you're mistaken. She knows that you'll be very rich, and maybe she wants her share.

Alan: So she's remained profoundly selfish. She has not been affected by the incredible planetary transformation that you mentioned earlier? Look, there's something contrived in your logic. You're not telling us the truth.

Hui: It seems obvious. Something is wrong with your explanation. You're trying to awake strong emotions in us to prevent us from thinking clearly. I therefore also agree with the principle of disobedience. We'll stay in the station until we are satisfied with your answers. You can call your replacement

75

team back. We'll not let them on board! You know very well that we can take manual control of the station. And if you really wanted to kill us, we would already be dead.

Houston: You're not serious. Do you know the cost of a rocket launch? Hui, considering you are commander, your attitude is tantamount to treason.

Hui: I think the rules have been extensively modified by your own doing. Moreover, I should remind you that it's not only the Russians have had a revolution. You wanted us to be united, so you should be satisfied. The ball is in your court. But do not take us for fools. We'll give you half an hour for discussion and consultation. Without a clear explanation from you, we'll take control of this lovely dwelling, the jewel of worldwide technology, and we'll prevent the replacement team from landing. You know, over the last 15 months we've had the time to get know the station pretty well. If you turn off the oxygen, we'll blow it up. Your actions also have a huge impact. In fact, don't forget Gavril's extra-lucid powers. You can't really hide anything from him!

A happy ending

The astronauts are seated around the table.

Hui: You're sure they can't hear us?

Gavril: Sure. They have the picture but no sound.

Alan: OK, we have to hide our mouths behind our hands, so they can't read our lips. Remember Hal in "2001, A Space Odyssey."

They put all their hands in front of their mouths.

Léa: And what if they send the GIGN?

Hui: What?

Léa: Special intervention team. I think it's called the Squat in the States. That's what we do in France when someone takes hostages.

Hui: We are in space. They can't blow a hole in the hull! They can't come if we don't open the door.

Gavril: What if there is no substitute team?

Alan: What are you suggesting?

Gavril: They can lie all down the line. If we don't trust them, it's all or nothing.

Alan: And why should they invent such a story?

Gavril:	To make us react. To make us believe they still have the ability to send rockets. There are many different possibilities.
Barisha:	What about my husband, could it be a bluff?
Gavril:	It must be considered.
Barisha:	Why do you think they would lie? Got an idea?
Gavril:	If they lie to us, it's because they are afraid of our reaction to the truth.
Alan:	And what if the TV programme never existed?
Hui:	What?
Alan:	Maybe they have invented this story to justify their silence during 15 months. Perhaps the disaster actually occurred and that it is now that the image of the Earth that's rigged.
Hui:	But in that case, why, from the outset, was the screen disguised as a window?
Gavril:	The answer is simple: to prevent the team from seeing what was really happening on Earth. We have only one solution. Someone has to do a space walk!
Barisha:	But none of us is entitled to do that. We didn't do the training. We don't know about the equipment.
Hui:	I think we're getting close to the an-

swer! Isn't it suspicious that no member of our crew has the ability to walk in space? This is the first time it's ever happened. I was well aware of this problem, but thought it didn't really matter. But I told myself that our mission was short lived and no space walk was planned.

Barisha: Gavril, you spent over a year in the Mir station and you never went out?

Gavril: No, never. I am an indoors man! When there was need work on the station, they brought in specialists. Guys who had undergone specific training. It's still a very dangerous thing to do! In space, you're moving at ten times the speed of a bullet. The smallest particle can pierce the suit. In addition, there's the risk of decompression sickness, like divers. That's why that part of the training is done in deep pools ...

Hui: Right! It now becomes clear that this is not a normal situation. I requested this training but I couldn't do it for some schedule reason. What about you Alan?

Alan: As you know, I was called in at the last minute to replace a colleague who died in a car accident. I didn't have the time.

Hui: And women are only very rarely trained.

Gavril: Which country built the part of the module that contains the window?

Hui: China. Why?

Gavril: I think the Chinese have taken control on Earth.

Alan: What did you say?

Gavril: Calm down, Alan and listen to me quietly. You are   the guardian of a secret that is more important than your own life, aren't you? (Silence) I must say that you have kept it perfectly. I could feel its presence but I've never been able to determine its nature. (Silence). You have been trained to protect this information in any circumstances, have you not? (Silence) So much so, that even now you can't admit its existence. (Silence). You say nothing but your silence speaks volumes. You were not prepared for such a situation.

Barisha: I don't understand. What are you talking about?

Gavril: Alan was the last defense weapon of the United States.

Hui: Was?

Gavril: And you, Hui? Were you unaware of your country's plans?

Hui: What? What are you talking about? Come on, spit it out.

Gavril: You went out into space to take the solar panels that you wanted to take back to

Earth?

Hui: No, not at all. I took the interior panels, those in the small solar module, attached to the translucent sheets.

Gavril: And did you look through those sheets?

Hui: No. I was too busy removing the panels as fast as possible. Then, once removed, I immediately replaced the inner metal wall, preventing anyone from noticing their disappearance. At that point, we didn't know that our main window was a screen.

Léa: Gavril, are you going to explain what you're getting at? Our half-hour will soon be over.

Gavril: Alan knows a code that can trigger the American nuclear space force, don't you Alan? (Silence) On receiving of a particular signal, or perhaps in the absence of this signal, he is supposed to trigger the world's most powerful strike force. (Silence) And where are those destructive warheads aimed? On China, of course, the only real threat to the New World Order run by the Americans since the fall of the Berlin Wall. (Silence) Alan is much more important to the United States than his personality suggests. Moreover, I believe he is unmarried and has no children. They would be too easy targets. (Silence) The history of the car accident is false, too. It just helped Alan keep out of sight until takeoff.

Léa: Is this true, Alan?

Alan is clearly embarrassed. His eyes move quickly from one person to another. He looks like a bomb about to explode.

Gavril: What I don't know, an important detail, is whether Alan was part of a plan of attack or of defence. The Chinese apparently knew about the U.S. strategy and decided to take control. They unleashed their nuclear attack on America and they made us believe in a natural disaster to neutralize the threat posed by Alan. It seems it took them 15 months to get Houston up and running again. But the Chinese still have a major concern and this concern is ... Alan! Alan remains their number one danger. He must still have power, otherwise we would not have been entitled to this reality show scenario. What bothers me is the simultaneous scheduled departure of Hui and Léa and the resumption of communications with Houston.

The tension is unbearable in the station. The astronauts survey one another like cowboys in a Western shootout. Who will move first? Finally, Alan starts speaking. His voice is unrecognisable, more sedate and serious. His nervousness has disappeared. His hands are still covering his mouth.

Alan: Bravo, extra-lucid Gavril. I would like to thank you for enlightening me on a number of points. So, here I am faced with a decision of great importance. Should we eliminate humanity? Or should I follow the advice of Bertrand Russell, the English philosopher who said "Better Red Than Dead?" America has in fact placed in this station a device for firing nuclear missiles located in space. If your assumptions are correct, my dear Gavril, I infer that the Chinese are not able to neutralize them. Not for one minute since the beginning of our adventure together, have I stopped thinking of the enormous responsibility that lies on my shoulders. Ever since the advent of the global disaster, I have doubted its real existence. I should have triggered the nuclear destruction process, as indeed I was not getting the correct signals from Earth. But with such a catastrophe of course, it seemed normal.

Alan gets up quietly, talking constantly, and moves slowly towards the window.

I must admit that at no time did I think that this window could be a screen. I spent hours with my nose up against it. It is an amazing device. (Pause)
With time, I learned to appreciate each one of you, but upon the resumption of communications with Houston, I knew everything was fake. Why did I not act immediately? Because I wanted to talk to you, once Hui was out of the way. That's why I hid the cameras. Hui's suicide took me by surprise. I thought it was a trick, but the angel's appearance reassured me, because I myself have been through a similar experience. Then I discovered this ...

He moves slightly to the left and presses simultaneously on two panels in the structure. This action opens a concealed door. Inside, there is a keypad on which he begins to type numbers. Suddenly, Gavril rushes at him, followed by Hui, slower in his movements. They catch Alan and bring him to the ground, but not before he has entered his code.

Alan: Too late, gentlemen. The signal is transferred. Did you really think that I could let the Chinese win? Can you imagine life on Earth without democracy, under the rule of the Communist Party, led by madmen who think they're God?

Barisha: You had no intention of consulting us.

Alan: Of course not! I suspected that you would not let me enter my code. It is obvious that the alleged substitute team's mission was to eliminate us. Hui is necessarily part of it. It would never have been possible to change the station's algorithms without the help of someone on the inside. And Hui it was who chose the moment to end our isolation, as you pointed out so well, Gavril. Thank you, again, for your information. It helped me make a difficult decision.

Léa: My God!

Alan: Actually, we are now in the same situation as before, but this time, we know each other a little better and there is no doubt about it. In a moment, all life on earth will be destroyed. Unless there is some divine intervention, of course.

84

THE END